For
Ma and Pa
with very much love

and, with grateful thanks,
to
the Walker "Moles" team
for their patience.
C.A.

First published 1994 by
Walker Books Ltd
87 Vauxhall Walk, London SE11 5HJ

This edition published 1997

2 4 6 8 10 9 7 5 3 1

Text © 1994 Richard Edwards
Illustrations © 1994 Caroline Anstey

This book has been typeset in Monotype Garamond.

Printed in Hong Kong

British Library Cataloguing in Publication Data
A catalogue record for this book is available
from the British Library.

ISBN 0-7445-5446-2

STANDARD LOAN

11. MAY 04
22. MAY 04

2 0 APR 2009
0 9 NOV 2009
2 6 OCT 2011

WITHDRAWN

MOLES CAN DANCE

Written by Richard Edwards

Illustrated by Caroline Anstey

WALKER BOOKS
AND SUBSIDIARIES
LONDON • BOSTON • SYDNEY

In the
warm wormy darkness
underground, moles were doing
their work. All day long they dug
tunnels and corridors and pushed up
mole-hills into the field above. It was
tiring work and the young mole soon
got bored. "I'm worn out," he said,
"and I'm all cramped up. I don't
like digging. I want to stretch.
I want to run about.
I want to …

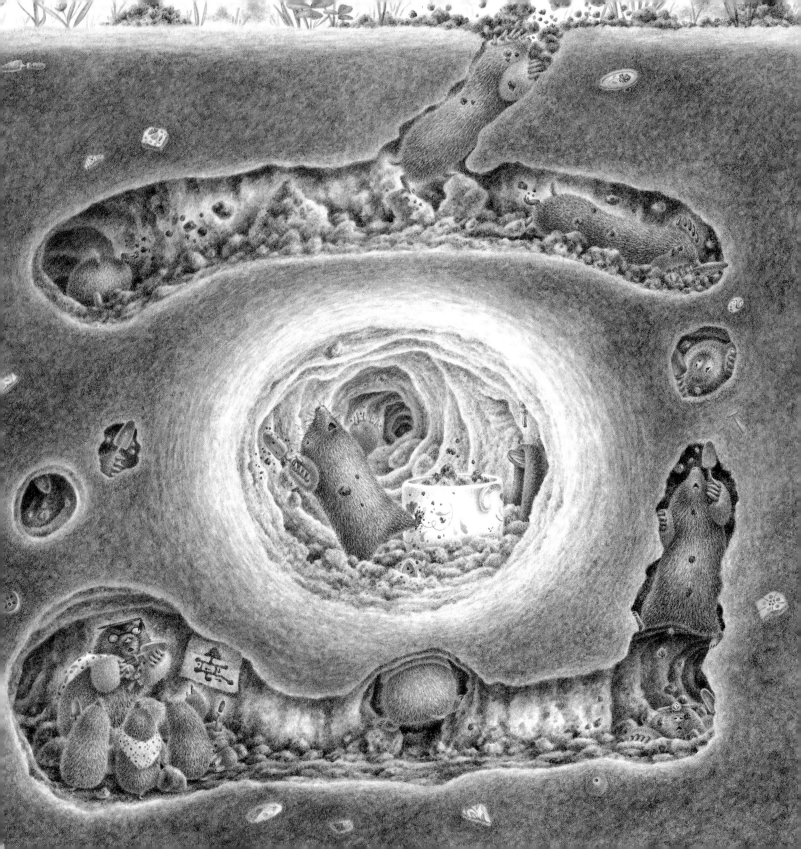

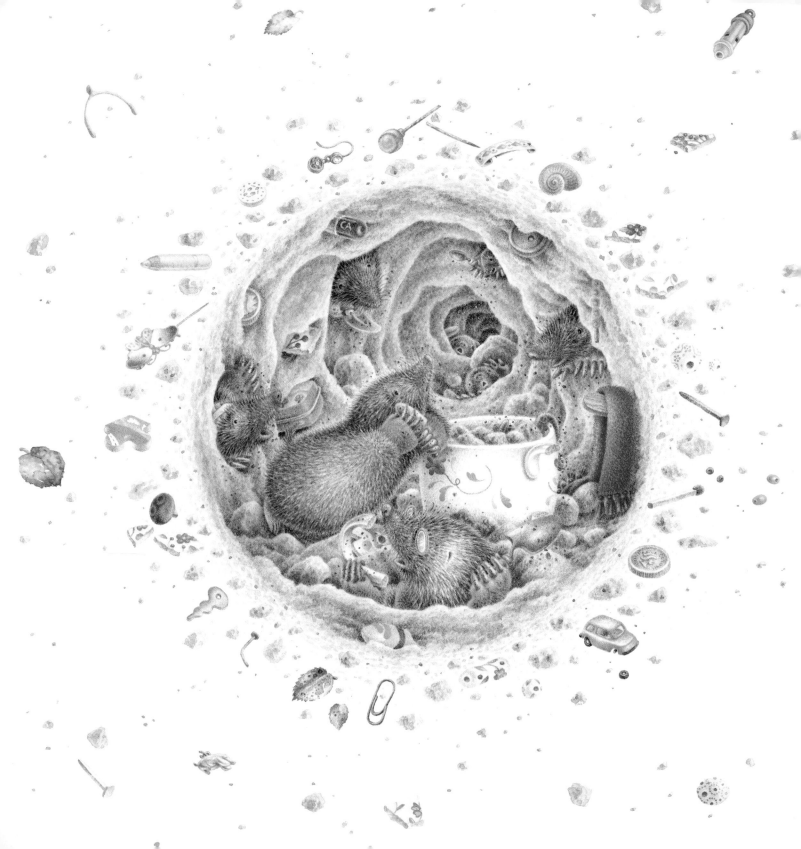

... *dance*!"

"Moles can't dance," said the old mole. "Moles aren't made for dancing, they're made for digging. Whoever heard of a mole dancing!"

"Moles can't dance," said all the other moles.

"See," said the old mole. "What did I tell you? Now stop being silly and dig that tunnel."

The young mole dug as he was told, but all the time he was thinking: I want to learn to dance. Why shouldn't I learn to dance? It's not fair.

Then he had an idea. If the moles couldn't
teach him to dance, perhaps someone else could.
Quickly he scrabbled his way upwards and broke
out into the dazzling sunshine of the field.

A cow was looking at him.

"I want to learn to dance," said the young
mole.

"I can't teach you," said the cow. "Cows can't
dance. They can chew grass and wave their
tails and moo, but they can't dance."

And it went on chewing grass.

The mole walked on and met a frog.

"I want to learn to dance," said the mole.

"I can't teach you," said the frog. "Frogs can't dance. They can hop about and swim, but they can't dance."

And it hopped into the pond and swam away.

Next the mole met a fox.

"I want to learn to dance," said the mole.

"I can't teach you," said the fox. "Foxes can't dance. They can prowl round the fields, keeping very quiet, but they can't dance."

And it went on prowling.

The mole walked on and saw a woodpecker
hammering at a tree.

"I want to learn to dance," called the mole.

"I can't teach you," said the woodpecker.
"Woodpeckers can't dance. They can fly from
tree to tree, bashing the bark with their beaks,
but they can't dance."

And it went on bashing.

Then the mole heard a funny noise coming
from behind a hedge.
THUMPA THUMPA THUMPA
What could it be?
THUMPA THUMPA THUMPA
The mole crawled into the hedge and looked
out on the other side. Two children were playing
in a garden. Dodge was making the
THUMPA THUMPA THUMPA by banging
on some boxes, and Daisy was dancing on
the grass. Real dancing!
The mole had never
seen anything
so fine in all
his life.

Dodge drummed  and Daisy
danced
and the mole watched carefully.

Daisy spun round on one leg
and the mole spun round on one leg.

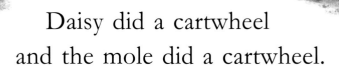

Daisy did a cartwheel
and the mole did a cartwheel.
Daisy hopped up and down and so did the mole.

Every step that Daisy danced,
the mole danced too, until shadows
began to creep across the garden.
"Better get back," said the mole to himself. "It's
getting late." And he turned and began
to dance his way home.

The woodpecker was
so surprised to see the mole
dancing back along the path
that it almost fell off its branch.

The fox was so surprised
to see the mole dancing
along the hedgerow
that it almost
toppled into
a ditch.

The frog was so
surprised to see the mole dancing
past the pond that it swallowed
a mouthful of muddy water.

The cow was so
surprised to see the
mole dancing across
the field that it
stood still for a long
time, with a grass
stalk sticking out
of its mouth.

"Where have you been?" asked the old mole.

"Just … dancing," said the young mole.

"Moles can't dance," said the old mole.

"Oh, yes they can," said the young mole.
"I'll show you." And he climbed on to the top of the nearest mole-hill and began to hop and spin about.

Soon all the other moles came up to see what was happening.

"He's dancing!" said one mole.
"And if he can, so can we.
    Come on!"

So, in ones and twos and
threes, they all began to dance.
Some on mole-hills, some on the
grass, some very badly, some very well,
some moles hopping, some moles jumping

and some moles spinning
around, but all of them, even
the old mole, having a fine time as
they danced and danced and danced and
danced by the light of the climbing moon.

MORE WALKER PAPERBACKS
For You to Enjoy

WUZZY TAKES OFF
by Robin and Helen Lester/Caroline Anstey

In this story featuring a classic Gund soft toy, Wuzzy, the woodland bear, sets off on a great adventure to the moon. To the reader, however, the "moon" may seem oddly familiar!

0-7445-5226-5   £3.99

THE MOON FROG
by Richard Edwards/Sarah Fox-Davies

The Moon Frog is just one of many memorable creatures in this entertaining volume of animal verse – some nonsense, some humorous, some poignant, all highly original and exquisitely illustrated.

"Wonderfully inventive poems with surefooted rhythms and a nice variety of form. Richard Edwards at his best."
The Daily Telegraph

0-7445-3161-6   £5.99

"QUACK!" SAID THE BILLY-GOAT
by Charles Causley/Barbara Firth

The animals all go crazy, when the farmer lays an egg! A brilliant comic rhyme by one of this country's leading poets, with funny pictures by the illustrator of the Smarties Book Prize Winner, *Can't You Sleep, Little Bear?*

"Very attractive ... very funny." *Parents*

0-7445-5246-X   £4.50

Walker Paperbacks are available from most booksellers, or by post from B.B.C.S., P.O. Box 941, Hull, North Humberside HU1 3YQ
24 hour telephone credit card line 01482 224626
To order, send: Title, author, ISBN number and price for each book ordered, your full name and address, cheque or postal order payable to BBCS for the total amount and allow the following for postage and packing:
UK and BFPO: £1.00 for the first book, and 50p for each additional book to a maximum of £3.50.
Overseas and Eire: £2.00 for the first book, £1.00 for the second and 50p for each additional book.
Prices and availability are subject to change without notice.